SandyBoy and His New Home
(A SandyBoy Adventure)

by Cindi Flow
illustrated by Judy Gaudet

SandyBoy and His New Home
(A SandyBoy Adventure)
by Cindi Flow
illustrated by Judy Gaudet

Published by

Texas Sisters Press, LLC
www.TexasSistersPress.com

©2021 Cindi Flow

ISBN: 978-1-952041-37-2 (Hardcover)
ISBN: 978-1-952041-38-9 (Paperback)
ISBN: 978-1-952041-39-6 (Ebook)

This book is dedicated to
my husband, Dick Flow,
who has always supported
my horse adventures!

"Hi, I am SandyBoy. Today is moving day. Have you ever left your home and moved to a new place?"

"Have you moved to a place you have never been before?"

"I am a litle scared, but I am also excited!"

"My owner is sad that I need a new home. There is some sickness in the family and she can no longer care for me, or ride me."

"I understand, but I am also sad. I will miss her and this farm."

4

"Time to go. Sometimes things happen that are both sad and happy."

"I hope this new farm will be my forever home."

"I am excited and nervous to meet my new owner and make new friends!"

"I like riding in the trailer. I like watching all of the houses and people we pass."

"I wonder if my new home is far away?"

The truck drove into the new farm.

"We have finally arrived."

When I backed off the trailer, I sniffed the air.
"Is that salt air I smell? What is that sound I hear?"

"Is it thunder? It's not raining."

"It is the ocean waves on the beach!
Am I going to live by the ocean? I am excited!"

"A girl came toward me. She was holding the biggest, orangest, carrot I ever saw!"

"When she came close, I saw she had the kindest brown eyes."

"She told me her name was Mia, and I would be staying on her farm from now on."

"She was very gentle as she fed me the carrot."

"I looked around and saw more horses out in the pasture. I am nervous about meeting them. I hope they like me."

"Have you ever worried about making new friends?"

Mia said, "It is time to move you into your new home! I hope you like our old barn, your stall, and your new neighbors!"

"This is such a huge, old barn. Mia told me it was built long ago, around 1757. That is really old!"

"It has been home to a lot of cows and horses over the years."

"Wow! This is a big stall with soft sawdust on the floor, and lots of yummy hay to eat."

"I am already feeling better about moving here."

"Soon, other horses were brought into the barn for the evening and to have their supper."

"I sniffed noses with my two neighbors, Nelson and Mija. They welcomed me with a soft nicker."

"My new owner, Mia, is right! I am going to have new adventures and make new memories here at Oceanview Farm."

"I am excited to be out in the pasture with the other horses at the farm."

"However, some of them are not very friendly."

"I don't understand why some of them put their ears back and run away from me."

"They don't even know me!"

"I think when they get to know me, we will all be friends. Sometimes, it just takes time to get to know each other."

"Has this ever happend to you in a new neighborhood or school?"

"Now that I have been here for a few days, Mia is going to walk me around the farm so I can see the different pastures and the riding ring."

"I think she might even take me to the beach! I cannot wait!"

"I have never been to the beach before. I am a little nervous! Look at all that water... and how it moves back and forth!"

"I do not want to walk in it. I am used to walking through puddles, but not these ripples and waves."

"I hope we just walk on the sand this time."

25

"Look! That bird does not look like any bird I have ever seen!"

"Mia tells me not to be afraid. It is a friendly seagull looking for a fish or crab to eat."

"It is time to go back home. This has been so much fun learning more about my new home, and getting to know Mia better."

"Maybe tomorrow, she will ride me. We can explore more!"

"We are going on a trail ride today. It feels good to have a saddle on again."

"Trail rides are so much fun! I hope Mia enjoys riding me."

"I am always very careful on the trails."

"I love summer. Look at those beautiful buttercups in the field waving in the wind... and those daisies!"

"I live in a beautiful place by the sea!"

"Oh my, what are those? I stopped to look."

"Mia said those are turkeys. They also live here on the farm."

"There are so many of them... big ones, and small babies!"

"They are not afraid of me, so I will not be afraid of them."

"On our way back to the barn, a large bird flew over us. It landed high up in a pine tree."

"That is a bald eagle," said Mia, "There are two of them that live here on the farm with us."

"I have so many new neighbors!"

"We had such a nice trail ride. I think Mia enjoyed our first ride together. I know I did!"

"We are back at the barn and the friendly barn swallows are zooming in and out."

"Sometimes, I think they will land on me, or fly into my stall!"

"I can hear the cries of the babies way up in their nests at the top of the barn."

"They are hungry, and I am, too!"

"After Mia took off my saddle and brushed me, she gave me the crunchiest red apple!"

"It was so good. I would have liked another one, but Mia said it was too close to my supper."

"She thought it would spoil my appetite, but I just love to eat!"

"How about you?
Do you like crunchy red apples?"

"What do I hear?"

"The welcome nickers of all the horses!"

"They ALL missed me!"

"I love my wonderful new owner and all my new friends."

"I am so happy to be living by the ocean!"

"I know there will be many new adventures for me to share with you!"

About the Author
Cindi Flow, Ed.D.

Cindi Flow's love of animals began as a young girl with her first pet dog and cat. Her best friend had a horse which they both rode and that instilled an early love of horses. However, once a grownup, career, marriage and parenting were the primary focuses of her life. Horses and reading were her passion. Reading stories about horses inspired her dream of one day having a special horse of her own. When she turned seventy years old, that dream became a reality. Cindi and her husband live in Maine with her dream horse, SandyBoy, a handsome Palomino gelding with a great heart who loves riding on the beach!

SandyBoy and Cindi are now focused on sharing the adventures of a horse friendship with children around the world. Sandyboy will inspire children to overcome obstacles in their lives and build their own dreams.

"Reading's A Ride! Bringing to Life One Adventure at a Time."

Keep up with Cindi and SandyBoy at CindiFlowWrites.com

About the Illustrator
Judy Gaudet

Judy Gaudet studied technical and medical illustration hoping to combine her career in microbiology with her lifelong love of art. Judy lives in southern Maine where she finds inspiration for her work in the landscapes, wildlife, and historic sites that surround her home.

CPSIA information can be obtained
at www.ICGtesting.com
Printed in the USA
BVHW020936190721
612309BV00005B/764